All children have
a great ambition to read
to themselves...

and a sense of achievement when they can do so.
The **read it yourself** *series has been devised to*
satisfy their ambition. Since many children learn
from the Ladybird Key Words Reading Scheme,
these stories have been based to a large extent
on the Key Words List, and the tales chosen are
those with which children are likely to be familiar.

The series can of course be used as supplementary
reading for any reading scheme.
Billy Goats Gruff is intended for children reading up
to Book 2c of the Ladybird Reading Scheme. The
following words are additional to the vocabulary
used at that level –

up, on, billy goats, Gruff, little,
middle-sized, big, eat, grass,
bridge, troll, under, over, trip,
trap, fat, him, splash

Published by Ladybird Books Ltd Loughborough Leicestershire UK
Ladybird Books Inc Auburn Maine 04210 USA

Printed in England (3)

Billy Goats Gruff

by Fran Hunia
illustrated by John Dyke

Ladybird Books

Here are
the billy goats Gruff.

This is
little billy goat Gruff.

He likes to jump.

This is
middle-sized
billy goat Gruff.

He likes
to have fun.

This is
big billy goat Gruff.

He likes
to eat grass.

11

Here is a bridge.

A big troll
has a home
under the bridge.

The billy goats Gruff
want to go
over the bridge
for some grass.

14

Trip, trap,
trip, trap, trip, trap.

Little billy goat Gruff
is on the bridge.

Up jumps the troll.

He says,
I want
to eat you up.

No, no, says
little billy goat Gruff.

Here comes
middle-sized
billy goat Gruff.

He is big and fat.

You can
eat **him**
up!

Yes, says the troll.
Yes, I can.

I can eat
middle-sized
billy goat Gruff,
says the troll.
You can go
over the bridge.

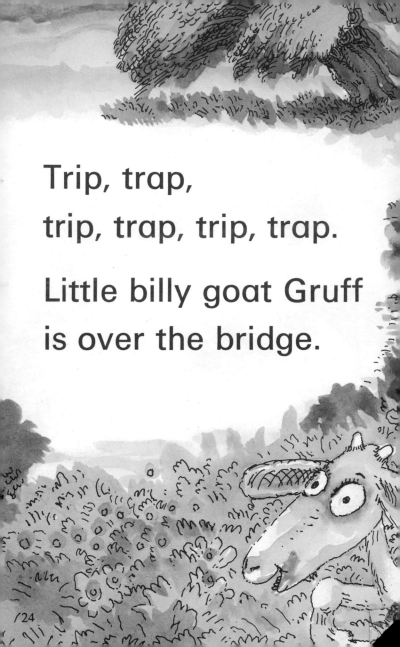

Trip, trap,
trip, trap, trip, trap.

Little billy goat Gruff
is over the bridge.

Middle-sized
billy goat Gruff
looks up.

Little billy goat Gruff
is over the bridge,
he says.

He has some grass
to eat.

I can go
over the bridge
for some grass.

Trip, trap,
trip, trap, trip, trap.

Middle-sized
billy goat Gruff
is on the bridge.

Up jumps the troll.

He says, I want
to eat you up.

No, no, says
middle-sized
billy goat Gruff.

Here comes
big billy goat Gruff.

He is big and fat.

You can
eat **him** up.

Yes, says the troll.

I can eat
big billy goat Gruff.

You can go
over the bridge.

Trip, trap,
trip, trap, trip, trap.

Middle-sized
billy goat Gruff
is over the bridge.

Big billy goat Gruff
looks up.

Little billy goat Gruff
and middle-sized
billy goat Gruff
are over the bridge,
he says.

I can go
over the bridge
for some grass.

Trip, trap,
trip, trap, trip, trap.

Big billy goat Gruff
is on the bridge.

Up jumps the troll.

He says,
I want to eat
you up.

No, no, says
big billy goat Gruff.
I want to eat
you up.

Up goes the troll.

He goes

SPLASH

into the water.

Trip, trap,
trip, trap, trip, trap.

Big billy goat Gruff
is over the bridge.

The billy goats Gruff
have fun in the grass.

They eat and eat
and eat.

We like it here,
they say.